C000132241

The Murder And Lynchi

The Book
The Movie
The Untold Story

Ernest J Muhammad

The Murder And Lynching Of Emmett Till:

The Book
The Movie
The Untold Story

ISBN
9780615970479

Emmett Till's murderers

Carolyn Bryant, her husband Roy, and his half-brother J.W. Milam

This book is dedicated to my mother Katherine, who gave me the foundation of my love for Jesus, The Christ. I also thank The Honorable Elijah Muhammad and The Honorable Minister Louis Farrakhan, who taught me how to love Black people unconditionally.

This is a revealing fiction book, based on the life of Emmett Louis Till (July 25, 1941- August 28, 1955) Emmett was murdered in Mississippi at the age of 14 after reportedly whistling with a White woman.

Till was from Chicago, Illinois, visiting his relatives in Money, Mississippi, in the Mississippi Delta region, when he whistled at 21-year-old Carolyn Bryant, the married proprietor of a small grocery store there.

Several nights later, Bryant's husband Roy and his half-brother J. W. Milam arrived at Till's great-uncle's house where they took Till, transported him to a barn, beat him, and gouged out one of his eyes, before shooting him through the head and disposing of his body in the Tallahatchie River, weighing it with a 70- pound cotton gin fan tied around his neck with barbed wire.

His body was discovered and retrieved from the river three days later. Reading the full details of what happened to Till and viewing photos in this book, is not for the faint of heart.

Table of Content

1
My Childhood

My Mother, Mrs. Mamie Till gave birth to me on July 25, 1941, in Chicago at Cook County Hospital. She named me Emmett Louis Till. My Daddy, whom I got my name from, tried to make it there for my birth, but he couldn't make it in time. The only person at the hospital besides Mama was Grandma. My Grandmother was a very strong – Mississippi churchgoing Black woman. She was right there by Mama's side every minute.

As it turns out, I was a breech baby. The doctors had to reach in and turn me around. I guess I gave Mama a hard time that day; I finally gave up and came out – all 8 pounds – 10 ounces of me.

My childhood was fun; Grandma took care of me for the most part, because my mother had to work long hours. I had cousins that lived in the suburbs; Wheeler, Simeon, and Ruthie, they would visit us quite often. We lived around 63rd and St. Lawrence, that's the Southeast side of Chicago.

We did the usual things that Black children did, like skateboarding. Back then, we made our own skateboards. To make one, just take a pair of skates and separate it into two halves. You would need a plank of wood to nail the two halves onto. Two wheels in the front and two on the back, and that's all you would need to make a skateboard.

Fun on wheels! On those hot Chicago days, we would get an old tire, put it around a fire hydrant with a two-by-four in front of the hole where the water comes out and cool off under the water spray.

All the children in the neighborhood would come to my block because I was the only one not afraid to get in trouble for turning on the fire hydrant.

Mama and Daddy separated and got a divorce in 1942. Daddy was well known as the "ladies man" around town; she caught him a few times with other women and just couldn't take it anymore. She even got a court order on him to stay away from her. He would try to choke her at times.

One time, he hit her and she responded by throwing some hot scalding water on him. As it turns out, he violated the court order many times, the judge gave him two choices; either go to jail or enlist in the army; he decided to go into the army. Later, Mama met a man named Mr. Bradley, they went on and got married. He was okay, at least he didn't hit her, but they only stayed together three years. I never knew why they didn't stay married.

I had an uncle named Moses Wright. He would visit us from Mississippi about twice a year. He would often say, "Mamie, when are you going to let the boy visit me in Mississippi?"

She would always respond, "He ain't ready for the South yet, I got to school him on what to say to White folks and what not to do." One day I asked her: "Mama, why do you need to teach me how to treat White folks, I already know what to say and do, don't I?"

2

The down south "white-folk talk"

That was the day when she finally gave me the "down south White folk talk." The conversation went something like this: "Emmett, you know that I love you with all of my heart, don't you?"
"Yes, Mama," I replied.

"When you love someone, you try your best to protect what you love. Emmett, I know that I taught you how to act around white folks here in Chicago, but the White folks in the South ain't like the ones here in Chicago, especially in Mississippi where your Uncle lives. I have decided to let you visit him this year, but you must listen to what I'm going to tell you, and follow my instructions to the letter. Do you understand me, boy?"

"Yes, Mama," I said in a very nervous voice.

"Emmett, there is good and bad in all people, Negro and White. There are some White folks that will help a Negro faster than your own folks will. One White person that did a lot of good was a man named John Brown. He gave his life helping slaves to freedom. I got some books about him that I will read to you later. The majority of Whites have a natural-born hatred for us, especially those in the south.

That's why I'm so afraid to send you down there. I will also tell you the story about one of the bravest slaves that ever lived. His name was Nat Turner. We can never thank God enough for what he did to those slave owners." "What kind of evil things did some White people in the south do to Negroes Mama?" I cried out.

"Baby, I'm just going to tell it to you plain. You're old enough now. I think you can take it. There are Whites out there that hate the very shadow that you cast. They don't want to have anything to do with you and wish that they could kill all Negroes, especially young males like you. Some wear police uniforms, some wear white collars and preach in church, and others wear white sheets over their heads and burn crosses, they call themselves the Ku Klux Klan."

"Why do they want to kill all Negroes, for what – what did we do?" I said, with a very puzzled look on my face.

"Let me start from the beginning my son when we were first brought over here as slaves. Son, when you refer to yourself, I want you to start using the term Black instead of Negro. Negro is a person made by the slave-master, it means something dead, Black means that you came directly from God Himself because He is a Black man."

"God is Black Mama?"

"Yes, He is Emmett, and so is Jesus."
"WOW!" I shouted, jumping up and down.
"I will explain that later when you get back
from Mississippi. For now, while you are
down south, use Negro until you get back
here, and I will fully explain it to you."

"Mama, what's a slave-master?"

"Sweetheart, there is much that you
should know that I have not told you, I
know they don't teach our true history in
school. It's my duty as a parent to teach
you the truth of our struggle as a people
here in North America."

"My last name and yours is Till, is that
right?"

"That's right Mama, it's because you
married Daddy." "Well...yes, and no. That
last name was forced on our people at the
time of slavery.

Emmett, our ancestors came from Africa. We were master builders, kings, and queens, living there in peace among one another. Your people built the White House and other large mansions here for Whites; they didn't know how to build anything like that for themselves.

To prove our people were so smart – when our ancestors were building the pyramids in Egypt, which is in Africa, White people were living in caves."
"Caves Mama?............"

"Yes Emmett, they stayed in the caves for about 2,000 years, until God sent a man named Moses to civilize them. They were walking on all fours like the other wild animals, eating raw-bloody flesh and eating the bark off trees. Years later, after Moses civilized them, they made boats and started sailing around to world, looking for someone to work for them as slaves.

A slave is a person who is the legal property of another person. They are forced to obey them as a 'master.'

They took us from our homeland Africa, forced us into their ships, put chains around our necks and legs, and killed anyone who didn't go along with the program. Some of our people didn't want to be slaves and just jumped into the Atlantic Ocean to be eaten by hungry sharks.

The sharks would actually follow the path of the ships, knowing that a meal of black bodies was guaranteed. It took 6 months for a slave ship to make the trip over here."

"How many years were we slaves, was it a long time?" I asked her, with tears in my eyes.

"Yes baby, It was a very long time, well over 350 years. I know it's hard for you to listen to this my son, don't cry Emmett, this is your history, and you must know this. When you have children, you must tell them the same story. It's important that we pass it on to each generation, regardless of how harsh the story is. The Italians pass on their history, the Irish, the Jews, and others make sure that everyone knows what happened to them, so why don't we?

At least others kept their own language, culture, and last names. We were stripped of everything – family names and language, we were left completely void! We don't even eat the same food as we did in Africa."

"Over 350 years, oh my God! Okay, Mama, please finish telling me our story," I said while wiping my eyes. "I want to know what happened to my people."

"Our people were in the bottom of the ships, together like sardines in a can. If someone next to you got sick, they got sick all over you. If you were a slave and had to relieve yourself, you did it on yourself and the person next to you, and this was going on among hundreds of slaves inside the ship, just think of the smell.

If someone died next to you, the body would decay with maggots all over them, and you. If a slave above you had to do the 'number 2,' the mess would fall down on your face and would stay on you for days sometimes weeks." "No Mama, Noooooooooooo!"

(Weeping profusely)

Yes, son, it's true, but that was the least of our worries. When we finally made it over here in the year 1555, we were sold to other Whites that owned cotton plantations. We made a lot of free money for them, that's why the slave master's children today are so well off. Totally free labor for hundreds of years.

The big companies that you see today are here because they worked our ancestors from 5 am in the morning, until 11 pm every day for free, all of those years. Whites were too weak and lazy to do it themselves: they had to get us to do the work for them. I have this book called "The Secret Relationship Between Blacks and Jews." I was surprised to find out that many of those who owned and sold us, were Jewish.

Emmett, just think if you had a lot of land, and you had 30-40 slaves to work the land for free as long as you lived, then passed the slaves to your offspring so that they could also get rich, and they did the same for their offspring. Now, do you see why they have everything and we have nothing?

Son, You know how we go to the store to buy clothes, shoes, or anything that you want to purchase?"

"Yes," I said while getting a little angry inside.

"Well, that's how we were bought and sold, like a pair of shoes or something. They would take us to something called a slave auction, where we were the merchandise to be sold, we had to call them master and not look them straight in the eyes.

Some slave masters were worse than others. Sons were forced to have sex with their own Mothers. Fathers were forced to have sex with their daughters. The slave master could just pick and choose any slave woman or girl that he wanted to be with, and in doing so, he gave slave women and girls many-many diseases.

Just for the fun and amusement, they would call a gathering of town folks to witness a slave hanging or a slave being burned alive. If a slave tried to escape by running away, the slave master would chop off his foot to teach him a lesson.

Some newborn babies of slaves would be thrown in the water for hungry alligators to eat, just for their enjoyment."

"Mama," I said in amazement, "how could anyone enjoy seeing a person being burned alive, or to see a baby being eaten by alligators? I don't understand – I just can't understand it – why.... why?

Forcing men to have sex with their own Mothers...this is far worse than what they taught us in school about what happened to the Jews in Germany with the Holocaust, much worse!

Over 350 years – it had to be more than 6 million of us killed during that time. I know I'm only 14 years old, but I can count."

"That's why I'm telling you these things Emmett because there are still a lot of white folks like that now, they have a sick disease called White superiority, they can't help themselves, it's how they were made, they will always believe that Whites are better than Blacks. They murdered more than 100 million of us from the time of slavery until now. You're right, I can also count Emmett. I'm not teaching you to hate anyone, son. I'm just telling you the truth of what happened to us as a people, nothing more – nothing less."

"Mother," I asked while pacing back and forth from the kitchen to the living room. "Why did God let this happen to us...couldn't He have stopped it? You taught me that God could do anything Mama!"

"Yes my child, God can do anything. He could have stopped it at any time. What we went through and what we are going through now is written in the Bible. It says that God's chosen people (Blacks) will be slaves in a land that is not their own, and they would serve a strange people in a strange land for 4 hundred years. Bring me my Bible son, it's right there on the coffee table.

Here, I'll let you read it – turn to the book of Genesis, chapter 15 – the 13th through the 15th verse. Read the Bible like I taught you son, with a strong man's voice. Stand up straight and stick your chest out, you're reading the words of God. Don't worry about that little stuttering problem you have, just let the Lord guide you son."

"Okay Mama, here it goes..."

"And.... he said unto Abram, Know of a.... surety that thy seed shall be a stranger........(stuttering)......... in a land that is not theirs, and shall serve them; and they shall afflict them four............ hundred years; And also that nation, whom they shall serve, will I judge: and.. (stuttering).....afterward, shall they come out with great substance. And thou shalt go to thy fathers in peace; thou shalt be buried in a.......... good old age."

"That was good Emmett, you did very well!"

(Clapping her hands)

"No people on earth fits this description of a lost people serving another people for that amount of time but us Emmett. Here is the good news my son; God said He would personally come to save us from those who tormented and kill us."

I started jumping for joy! "Wow Mama, God is coming Himself to save us?"

"Yes, baby – yes, He is coming back with Jesus! Emmett, I have one last thing to tell you before you go down south, and this is ONLY while you are there. When you speak to a White person, and I mean ANY White person – man, woman, or child, always address them as yes Ma'am or yes Sir. And never look them directly in the eyes. DO I MAKE MYSELF CLEAR SON!!!"

"Yes Ma'am, I understand."

"Are you sure you understand? This is very important; it's a matter of life and death. I know that I have taught you the very opposite about looking someone straight in the eyes while talking to them, but that's just for Chicago."

"I'll do just like you tell me Mom, don't worry."

"Okay, if it is the will of God, you will be leaving next month for Mississippi."

"Thank you, Mama," I said while giving her a big wet sloppy kiss on her left cheek. "I love you."

"You will be traveling on the train that stops at 63 rd street. You can only stay for 2 weeks; that should be long enough. Uncle Mose needs someone to keep him company, I'm sure he gets bored living all alone in that big old house. Your cousin Simeon will be there with you to play with."

(Doorbell ringing)

"Emmett, please see who is at the door."

"Okay, Mama............It's Mrs. Thompson." I was always glad to see her. Mrs. Thompson was Mama's best friend who lived across the street from us. She would always bring over some fresh baked goods like cookies, pound cake, or peach cobbler, she makes the best peach cobbler, Mrs. Thompson makes hers with fresh peaches – not the ones from the cans. Last year her husband and daughter were killed in a car accident on the Outer Drive. After the accident, she and Mama became best friends.

"Pearl, how are you doing? Come on in and have a seat."

"Girl, I got some chocolate chip cookies for you and Emmett. Mamie, are you sure that boy is only 14 years old, that boy is standing tall like a man."

"He's growing up fast Pearl, eating me out of house and home. Emmett usually goes with me to the grocery store; he makes sure I pick up all of his favorites, Oxtails, whole chickens, and turkey legs. Of course, I don't need to buy him any sweets, I leave that up to you. He's going to Mississippi next month to visit his Uncle."

"Girl, did you give him "the talk" yet? You know how those White folks are in Mississippi. A city boy can get into a lot of trouble down there girl! I had a cousin named Lee that went there 4 years ago, and we haven't seen him since. I believe in my heart the Klan got a hold of him."

"Pearl, now you know I ain't sending my only baby down there without schooling him on what to say and do. In fact, we just finished talking about that very thing just before you came to the door. I put my faith in the Lord Jesus; it's in His hands. I taught Emmett how to call on the name of Jesus! I know that you call on the Lord quite often."

"You are so right girl, I call on Him before going to bed – when I wake up and all during the day, I can't make it without Him in my life. As for my loss, time heals all wounds, I hope that you will never have to feel the pain of losing a loved one, it hurts so bad.

Thank you for your concern; you have been a true friend to me over these years Mamie. I thank God for you and Emmett. I believe Emmett will have a lot of fun in the south. He needs to be exposed to something else besides the big city life here in Chicago."

"Mamie, you know today while I was out shopping, I ran into one of those Muslims selling the Muhammad Speaks paper. I tried to get away but he kept at me until I finally brought one from him. He also sold me a copy of this book by The Hon. Elijah Muhammad. 'Message to the Blackman in America.'

I started reading it, and couldn't put it down until I finished the whole book. You and Emmett have a seat. I'm going to read a few pages from the book right now. I think that your son should definitely listen before going to the south."

3
Reading "Message To The Blackman In America"

God is a man and we just cannot make Him other than man, lest we make him an inferior one; for man's intelligence has no equal in other than man. His wisdom is infinite; capable of accomplishing anything that his brain can conceive.

A spirit is subjected to us and not we to the spirit. Habakkuk uses the pronoun "He" in reference to God. This pronoun"He" is only used in the case when we refer to a man or boy or something of the male sex. Are we living in a material universe or a "spirit" universe?

We are material beings and live in a material universe. Would not we be making ourselves fools to be looking forward to see that which cannot be seen, only felt? Where is our proof for such a God (spirit) to teach that God is other than man? It is due to your ignorance of God, or you are one deceived by the devil whose nature is to mislead you in the knowledge of God.

You originally came from the God of Righteousness and have the opportunity to return, while the devils are from the man devil (Yakub), who has ruled the world for the past 6,000 years under falsehood, labeled under the name of God and His prophets.

The worst thing to ever happen to the devils is: the truth of them made manifest that they are really the devils whom the righteous (all members of the black nation) should shun and never accept as truthful guides of God!

This is why the devils have always persecuted and killed the righteous. But the time has, at last, arrived that Allah (God) will put an end to their persecuting and killing the righteous (the black nation). I and my followers have been suffering cruel persecution – police brutality for the past 34 years; but have patience, my dear followers, for release is in sight. Even those who made mockery of you shall be paid fully for his or her mockery; for the prophecy of Habakkuk is true if understood; wherein he says, "Thou wentest forth for the salvation of Thy people" (the so-called Negroes) 3:13.

Never before this time did anyone come for the salvation of the so-called Negroes in America, whose rights have been ignored by their enemies (the white race) for 400 years. Now it is incumbent upon Allah to defend the rights of his lost-found helpless people, called Negroes by their enemies.

The whole of the third chapter of Habukkuk is devoted to the coming and work of God against our enemies and our deliverance. We must not take our enemies for our spiritual guides lest we regret it. You are already deceived by them. Why seek to follow them and their evil doings?

If I would say that God is not man, I would be a liar before him and stand to be condemned. Remember! You look forward to seeing God or the coming of the "Son of Man" (a man from a man) and not the coming of a "spirit." Let that one among you who believes God is other than man prove it!

One of the greatest handicaps among the so-called Negroes is that there is no love for self, nor love for his or her own kind. This not having love for self is the root cause of hate (dislike), disunity, disagreement, quarreling, betraying, stool pigeons, and fighting and killing one another.

How can you be loved, if you have not love for self? And your own nations and dislike being a member of your own, then what nation will trust your love and membership. You say of yourself, "I love everybody." This cannot be true. Love for self comes first. The Bible, the book that you claim to believe, says, "Love the brotherhood" (I Peter 2:17), "Love one another" (John15:17). Love of self comes first. The one who loves everybody is the one who does not love anyone.

This is the false teaching of the Christians for the Christians war against Christians. They have the Bible so twisted by adding in and taking out of the truth that it takes only God or one whom God has given the knowledge of the Book to understand it. The Bible puts more stress upon the "love for thy neighbor" than the "love for the brother." When asked "Who is my neighbor?" The answer was contrary and incorrect. Jesus' answer was that of two men who were on a journey.

They were not from the same place. One was from Jerusalem, the other one was a Samaritan.

The Samaritan came to where the man from Jerusalem lay wounded by the robbers who had stripped him of his possessions. The Samaritan showed sympathy for the fellow traveler. (He was not a neighbor in the sense of the word. A neighbor can be an enemy.) Many enemies live in the same neighborhood of a good neighbor. But, the answer that Jesus gave was a futile one which can be classified as a parable of the so-called Negroes and their slave masters.

The so-called Negroes fell into the hands of the slave-masters, who have robbed, spoiled, wounded, and killed them. The Good Samaritan here would be the Mahdi (Allah)-God in Person, as He is often referred to by the Christians as the "the second coming of Jesus, or the Son of Man to judge man."

This one will befriend the poor (the so-called Negroes) and heal their wounds by pouring into their heads knowledge of self and others and free them of the yoke of slavery and kill the slave-masters, as Jehovah did in the case of Pharaoh and his people to free Israel from bondage and the false religion and gods of Pharaoh. There were many other proofs in the Bible that agree with the above answer.

Love yourself and your kind. Let us refrain from doing evil to each other, and let us love each other as brothers, as we are the same flesh and blood. In this way, you and I will not have any trouble in uniting. It is a fool who does not love himself and his people. Your black skin is the best, and never try changing its color. Stay away from intermixing with your slave-master's children. Love yourself and your kind. Why do I stress the religion of Islam for my people, the so-called American Negroes?

First, and most important, Islam is actually our religion by nature. It is the religion of Allah (God), not a European organized white man's religion. Second, it is the original, the only religion of Allah (God) and His prophets. It is the only religion that will save the lives of my people and give them divine protection against our enemies. Third, it dignifies the black man and gives us the desire to be clean internally and externally and for the first time to have a sense of dignity.

Fourth, it removes fear and makes one fearless. It educates us to the knowledge of God and the devil, which is so necessary for my people. Fifth, it makes us to know and love one another as never before.

Sixth, it destroys superstition and removes the veil of falsehood. It heals both physical and spiritual ills by teaching what to eat when to eat, what to think, and how to act.

Seventh, it is the only religion that has the divine power to unite us and save us from the destruction of the War of Armageddon, which is now.

It is also the only religion in which the believer is really divinely protected. It is the only religion that will survive the Great Holy war, or the final war between Allah (God) and the devil. Islam will put the black man of America on top of civilization. So, why not Islam? Some people say, "Why so much religion?"

It is very necessary for me to teach the knowledge of that which is the only key to the hereafter for his brother. I will say here that this alone is salvation to you and me, just learning to love each other as brothers. Islam, unlike Christianity, is doing this right in your midst.

Regardless of how long and how hard you try to be a good Christian, you never have a sincere true love for your own black brother and sister as you should. Islam will give you true brothers and sisters the world over. This is what you need. A people subjected to all kinds of injustice need to join Islam. You are sure of Allah's (God) help in Islam.

Why don't the preachers of my people preach Islam? If they would, overnight they would be on top. Are you too proud to submit to Allah and sit in heaven while you live and have His protection against your open enemy? Take it or leave it. You will soon wish you had taken Islam. God is drying America up by degrees. This time is at hand, and hell is kindling up. Islam is the right way. (Reprinted from "Message To The Blackman in America" by Elijah Muhammad)

4
Four Little Girls

"Good morning Emmett, how are you today? You know you're going to a new school when you go back in September. How do you feel about being a freshman?"

"Good morning Mama, I'm okay. These summer breaks don't last long enough; they should last 6 months long (smiling). You know it's funny Mama, I'm going to be a freshman at the same high school that you went to 100 years ago, Wendell Phillips."

"Okay, I see you got jokes this morning young man - very funny. When you get to be my age, we'll see how you feel. Back then, Black folks could only attend 3 different high schools in Chicago, and Phillips was one of the three.

They didn't let us go to school in the White areas. Son, turn the radio up, I heard something about a special report."

"Okay, mom. Are we still going to church today?"

"Be quiet Emmett, I'm trying to listen to the radio."

Radio announcer:

This is a CBS special report – Ladies and Gentlemen, a terrible thing has just happened in Birmingham. A bomb from a speeding car was thrown into the 16th street Baptist church today killing four young Negro girls while they were in Sunday school class.

The girls have been identified as Carole Robertson, Cynthia Morris, Addie Mae Collins – all 14 – and 11-year-old Denise Mc Nair. A fifth victim, Sarah Collins, who is the younger sister of Addie Mae was not killed but lost an eye in the blast.

"OH MY GOD EMMETT!!!"

Radio announcer:

Two White Ku Klux Klan members, who have been known in 12 other recent Negro church bombings were picked up by police, questioned, and then later released. FBI Director J. Edgar Hoover has blocked the prosecution of the suspects by withholding evidence, saying the chance of winning a conviction was "remote."

Two Negro males: Johnny Robinson, 16, and a 13- year-old youth named Virgil Ware were also killed by Birmingham police when riots occurred after the church bombing. They were said to be throwing bricks at passing cars with White occupants. Gov. George Wallace has called in at least 300 State Troopers and 500 National Guardsmen.

The Rev. Dr. King has called President Kennedy assuring him that he will go to Birmingham to plead for a nonviolent reaction, and for Negroes not to riot...Just a minute ladies and gentlemen, we are about to bring you, Dr. King, at a live press conference on the church bombing. Here he is...

Dr. King Speaking:

Today in Birmingham, four little girls were murdered in cold blood by the Klan. Parents outliving their children is unheard of. Unheard of only if you are Negro and living in the south. Vicious white terrorists with hatred in their hearts for us threw a bomb into them 16th street Baptist church killing four innocent little girls in the holy house of God. Knowing full well that it was children's day at the church.

I once imagined a world where Negro children and white children would be able to hold hands and play together, but it seems that my hopes were only a "dream" deferred. This kind of killing has changed my mind forever. I no longer believe that the two races can ever live together in peace. There has been too much carnage, mass murder, and outright slaughter of my people without any remorse since the year 1555 when the first slaves came to these shores of America, hell-on-earth.

To date, no white man has ever gone to jail for the murder of a Negro, even in the face of full evidence. A White man's heaven is indeed a Negro man's hell. This terrorist bombing has now forced me to join hands with the Nation of Islam under the guidance of the Most Hon. Elijah Muhammad. I never thought that I would admit this, but Mr. Muhammad has been right all along.

The white man must be the devil that the Bible is talking about! Many others share this view, Gandhi of India, the Native Americans, who were murdered wholesale, The Aborigines of Australia who suffered the same, the Mexicans, the Asians, and the list goes on.

When there were no dark folks around for them murder, as in Germany, they killed 6 million of their own. Whites are the most blood-thirsty folks I have ever seen. In our 5 hour meeting, Elijah

Muhammad and I both came to an agreement that the teachings of Jesus are not the problem, but injecting the White man's made-up version of "Christianity" is – and always has been the problem of the Negro.

These false teachings of our tormentors have caused us to become impotent and weak as a people – unable to solve our social, political, and economic ills. Mr. Muhammad and his followers don't have these kinds of problems.

They are successful in every endeavor they put their minds on. They are builders of a nation – within a nation and no Caucasian dare lay hands on him. This is the kind of man I want to become – fearlessness and feared by my enemies. Uncompromising!!

Brothers and Sisters, we have been unsuccessful because we have been praying to the wrong God. He is not white – the real God is Black! Under deep reflection, meditation and conviction. I hereby renounce and denounce the White man's made-up religion Christianity and have accepted Islam as my religion under the guidance of The Honorable Elijah Muhammad!

I know that many of my followers will take issue with this decision to join forces with Mr. Muhammad. I see no other way now but the total separation of the races - the Black man doing for himself and the White man doing for himself. Mr. Muhammad has already proved that the Negro can live inside of America being totally independent.

Let me give you a good example of what I'm trying to convey:

If there is a married couple, whereas the man is constantly beating and abusing his wife, she would be an absolute fool to say: "I'm just going to stay with my husband and practice nonviolence. All of my real teeth are gone because he knocked them out. I only have vision in my left eye because he hit me in the right eye with a pipe wrench. I wear a wig all the time because he set fire to my real hair and burned my scalp."

You would have to agree with me that this woman is either mentally unstable, or she just loves torture. Well, this is how we have become as a people with our dealings with what now appears to me to be an open enemy of the Negro.

The whole entire world looks at us as insane for trying to love those who slaughter us on a daily basis. It's no different from the story of the married woman. We need a DIVORCE! And we need it NOW!

Unfortunately, I must apologize to my people, because I have been contributing to this "bad marriage" by inoculating the Negro with the wrong tractable type of religion – not the actual teachings of Jesus, no I'm not talking about that.

I'm talking about the way they forced on us their type of thralldom religion during slavery. When a marriage has irreconcilable differences, the man and woman will both agree that it is better to separate.

"YES, I NOW WANT TOTAL SEPARATION OF THE RACES!"

Mr. Muhammad, by the grace of God, has come up with an economic blueprint for us. This plan is not something that needs to be tried or tested; it is already working for the thousands of Muslims and non-Muslims under his guidance. Let me explain this wonderful program to you exactly the way the Honorable Elijah Muhammad taught it to me during our meeting.

"Emmett, turn the radio up, I want to hear this!"

Dr. King:

There are 5 basic steps to the economic program:

1. Recognize the necessity for unity and group operation (activities).

2. Pool your resources, physically as well as financially.

3. Stop wanton criticisms of everything that is Black-owned and Black-operated.

4. keep in mind – jealousy destroys from within.

5. Observe the operations of the White man. He is successful. He makes no excuses for his failures. He works hard in a collective manner. You do the same.

Mr. Muhammad also said to me:

"If there are six or eight Muslims with knowledge and experience of the grocery business – pool your knowledge, open a grocery store-and you work collectively and harmoniously, Allah will bless you with success. If there are those with knowledge of dressmaking, merchandising, trades, maintenance – pool such knowledge.

Do not be ashamed to seek guidance and instructions from the brother or sister who has more experience, education, and training than you have had. Accept his or her assistance. The White man spends his money with his own kind, which is natural. You, too, must do this. Help to make jobs for your own kind.

Take a lesson from the Chinese and Japanese and go give employment and assistance to your own kind when they are in need. This is the first law of nature. Defend and support your own kind. True Muslims do this.

Because the so-called American Negro has been deceived and misled, he has become a victim of deception. He is today in the worst economic condition of North America. Unemployment is mounting, and he feels it most. He assisted in reducing himself to his present insecure economic condition.

You, the Black man, are the only members of the human race that deliberately walk past the place of business of one of your own kind, and spend your dollars with your natural enemy. The so-called American Negro has never in the history of America been known to boycott or criticize the White man as he does his own kind.

He thus shows love for his enemy and hatred for his own kind. A true Muslim would never boycott the place of business of his fellow Muslim or Black brother. A true Muslim is proud of the success of his Black sisters and brothers. He recognizes that their success is his success. He recognizes the law of Islam. If one brother has a bowl of soup you have half of that soup."

(Reprinted from "Message to the Blackman in America," 1965.)

Dr. King continues:

This is why the Muslims are so successful. They pool their resources together and become prosperous. I'm calling for a march on Washington D.C., where I will introduce the program of Muhammad to all Negroes who are willing to listen and accept! I will now state some of the accomplishments of the Muslims under this program:

1. Thousands of acres of farmland
2. A Bank at 6760 s. Stony Island
3. Clothing stores: men and women
4. Grocery stores, bakery and coffee shops
5. The Salaam Restaurant on 8300 and Cottage Gr.
6. Importing thousands of pounds of fish/week 7. Selling millions of copies of Muhammad Speaks 8. Hundreds of housing units
9. A brand-spanking-new executive jet airplane 10. A giant Goss Urbinate newspaper press
11. A $2 Million dollar office building on S. Cottage Gr.
12. Their own schools M.U.I. across the U.S.

We would be totally independent of the White man within 5 years or less. God willing I will explain more at the march. The date of the march will be August 28th. I will be looking forward to seeing all of you there. Thank you and goodbye.

"Wow Emmett, did you hear what Dr. King just said? He said that he is no longer a Christian and has become a Muslim follower of the Honorable Elijah Muhammad and he wants total separation of the races. I can't believe it – I can't believe he just said that! I can just imagine what the newspaper headlines will say tomorrow."

5
Move To The Back Of The Bus

Before Mama would let me take the long trip down south to Mississippi, she had me to do a "dry-run" of traveling by myself. She had a nice powdered blue formal dress on layaway downtown at Marshall Fields that she wanted me to pick up out of the layaway.

I would need to take three different buses to get there. My mother told me to keep my mouth shut, respect my elders and always sit towards the rear of the bus because that's where Negroes were supposed to sit.

Well, everything was going alright until I got on the third bus. A Negro woman who appeared to be around 40 or 45 years old got on and sat right at the very first seat on the bus. An elderly woman sitting next to me said in a worried voice, "O my God, is she insane?"

The bus driver looked at her with the evilest face I have ever seen. He put on the parking brakes, turned to his right, and said, "Don't you know where you belong lady? Get your Black ass to the back of the bus now, and I mean right now!"

I could feel the fear in the air from all the riders, White and Negro. Inside the bus was a dead silence. The woman just sat there looking straight forward. The bus driver, now turning red as an apple, got up out of his seat, put his face down even with hers, eye-to-eye and shouted directly in her face; "listen, you black monkey-nigger bitch, this is the last time I'm going to say this – go to the back of the bus right fucking now, or you're going to jail!" The lady next to me started crying, saying, "Lord Jesus please...."

The woman said to the bus driver in a stern voice, "I paid 25 cents just like the other White folks that got on this bus, I deserve to sit in any seat on this damn bus as I please!"

Now it seems like everything was going in slow motion. The bus driver raised his hand as high in the air as he could, he came down swiftly with all five fingers spread and slapped her right in the face at full strength.

She fell to the floor, brushed herself off, got back up, and put her broken glasses back on. She then sat right back in the same seat. The bus driver snatched her purse, went through it, and found an ID card.

A police car was passing by, the officer saw a lot of people standing around the bus, and came inside. The policeman said to the driver, "Hey Jim, what's going on, what's all the commotion about?

Your bus is causing a big traffic jam out here buddy."

"This nigger bitch refuses to go to the back of the bus, here's her ID. Get her the hell off my bus now Frank before I halfway kill her."

"Let me see the ID.....hmmm.....Mrs. Rosa Parks, do you understand that you are breaking the law on this bus today? Colored in the back – Whites in the front. You got glasses on, the sign is right here in front of your face."

She just sat there, holding the left side of her bruised face, and said, "It's just not fair – it ain't fair that we pay the same amount of money as Whites and can't sit in the seats that we want to sit in. Plus, I pay city taxes."

"Mrs. Parks," The officer said. "My friend James Blake is a very well respected bus driver, he's been driving for 22 years.

Now the law is the law, and I am here to enforce it. You should be glad that we even let your kind ride on the same bus as us whites. If it was up to me, the bus would be segregated just like we do the water fountains, one bus marked for Colored only – and one for whites.

Now get your black ass to the back of the bus with the other law-abiding Negroes, or I will be forced to take you to jail. You don't want me to do that, do you?" She looked him straight in the eyes, without blinking, and said, "do what you have to do officer!"

The officer put handcuffs on the lady and took her off the bus. I hope they didn't hurt her anymore. Mama ain't going to believe this when I get home.

6
Home From Downtown Chicago

I picked up the daily newspaper that my friend Tony delivered to our door. I always wanted to be a paperboy. Tony makes pretty good money. Mama was so proud of me, she gave me a big hug, and said: "I'm so proud of my little man. Emmett, you went downtown all by yourself, got my new dress out of layaway, and made it back home safe. I think you're ready to make the trip to Mississippi." She gave me another big hug.

Before I gave her the newspaper, I tried to impress her by reading the headlines. I stumbled a little, reading to myself first – Civil R....ights Wo....rker Slain.

"Mama, what's a Civil Rights Worker?"

"That's a person that helps poor folks like us when White folks don't treat us right. You know, like Dr. King. Why do you ask?"

"Does Slain mean dead?"

"Boy give me that paper, let me see what you talking about!"

"Mama, first can I tell you about what happened on the bus today..........it was this Black lady...she sat in the......."

"Emmett, I don't want to hear about some woman on the bus, give me the paper like I asked, thank you!"

"But Mama.......She sat in the front......"

"Oh my God, the KKK killed Medgar Evers, I knew it was only a matter of time before they got him. This is so sad, Emmett. That man did nothing but good for Colored and whites, now he's dead. When will they ever stop killing our men and boys, It makes no sense at all. I feel so sorry for his wife Myrlie!" (weeping)

"Mama, are they going to kill Dr. King?"

"I doubt that they would do something that crazy Emmett, Negroes would act a complete fool. Every city in America would be up in flames -no son, they don't want that – they don't want him dead, that's one man they want to keep very much alive."

7

The Final Departure
August 20, 1955
The day of departure from the
63rd Street Illinois Central Train Station

Today is the day I leave for Mississippi. Mom and I just arrived at the 63rd St. train station. The train should be here in about 20 minutes. She just kept staring at me, like she wasn't going to see me again.

"How do you feel son? Are you a little nervous?"

"I'm okay, not nervous at all Mom, you seem more nervous than me. I got Daddy's ring on and shined it up. I'm going to show it off to the girls down south."

"Baby, give me that ring. You don't need to be wearing that, I forgot he gave that ring to you."

"Please Mama can I wear it? The girls love it, I'll make the fellas jealous. This ring is a girl catcher. I'm 14 now, it's time I got myself a little woman."

"Boy, leave those little fast-tail girls alone. They ain't nothing but trouble. The only thing you need to be worried about is the talk that we had back at home about how to act around southern white folks.

If you see a sign saying for whites only, like a water fountain or restroom, make sure you stay far away from those and use the one that say ``Colored only on it............okay."

"I already know that, I'll be all right. I ain't saying nothing to them but yes Sir - no Sir or yes Ma'am and no Ma'am, and I won't look them straight in the eyes, I'll look down to the ground. See mom, I got it."

"Emmett..........I love you" (crying)

"I love you too Mama, stop all that crying. You're trying to make me stay in Chicago with you, aren't you?"

"No son, that's not why I'm crying. I'm shedding tears because for once, when I look in your big brown eyes, I no longer see that little boy anymore – I see a man! A strong handsome man just like your father. You just might get all of the girls down there."

(Mother and son embrace while the train whistle is heard in the background. Emmett takes his hand and wipes her tears.)

I gave mom a kiss, told her that I love her, and got on the train. As I looked out of the train window, she was waving goodbye with one hand, and had tissue in her other hand, blowing her nose with it and crying. Mom packed a big lunch for me, some fried chicken, three turkey sandwiches, 2 apples, and one orange. Cold chicken on a long trip is the best chicken you can eat.

Soon, the sound of the train wheels – click-clack-click-clack-click-clack, put me straight to sleep, it must have been 2 hrs or more. When I woke up, the seat that was vacant next to me when I got on the train, was now occupied by an elderly white lady. I thought to myself, this car is for Coloreds only, why is this white woman in the third-class car. And why is she sitting next to me when there are other empty seats around?

"Well hello there young man, how are you doing?" The woman said. "You did some heavy snoring, much louder than the train tracks. (smiling) What's your name?"

Wiping the sleep from my eyes, I muttered: "Hello Ma'am my name is Emmett."

"That's a wonderful name. My name is Mrs. Bergstein, pleased to meet you

Emmett – And why is Mr. Emmett on the train all by himself, where are mom and dad, does Mr. Emmett have a last name, and how old are you?"

"Yes, Ma'am, my last name is Till, I'm 14 years old. I live in Chicago with my Mother. She's sending me down to Money, Mississippi on summer vacation to visit my uncle."

"That's exactly where I'm going, good I'll have someone to talk with along the way, I'm by myself as well. I'm actually in the 1 st class car. The porters are cleaning up a mess some kids made, then I go back. Emmett, Have you ever sat in 1st class?"

"No Ma'am."

"You want to go?"

"No Ma'am, I'm okay here, thanks."

"Emmett, my family owns over half of this train company. I'm the boss on this train and I insist that you be my guest in 1st class. What kind of lunch did your mom pack for you?"

"Some fried chicken and turkey sandwiches."

"Well, guess what, in 1st class, you can eat steak, lobster, shrimp, duck, lamb, and most anything you want."

"Do they have chocolate malts in 1 st class?" I asked grinning ear-to-ear.

"They sure do, " she said, looking at me over the top of her glasses. Come on, let's go. The porters should be finished by now. Emmett, why are you looking down to the floor when you speak to me, my face is up here? Oh, I know, your mom told you to do it for going down south, right?"

"Yes, Ma'am, she did. She said doing it will keep me out of trouble with White folks."

"Well, while you're with me, you don't need to do that young man, but as soon as we get to Mississippi, you do exactly as she told you. Yeah, unfortunately, you have to do it."

"Yes, Ma'am"

Mrs. Bergstein was the nicest lady I have ever known. When she took me to the 1 st class car, everyone was looking at us like they saw a ghost or something. I guess Negroes don't come to cars like this one. All the seats were red velvet and the lights were chandeliers.

Everyone knew her, and they all looked rich-very rich. She took my lunch bag, gave it to one of the porters, and told him to throw it away. He then came back with a large plate with steak, lamb, a baked potato, and broccoli. She took a napkin and put it in my lap. I didn't know how to cut up the steak, so she did it for me.

"Slow down young man, the steak ain't going to leave your plate. Are you going to have enough room for that chocolate malt?" (smiling) "Emmett, have you ever tried one of these, they are simply delicious?"

"Yes, I eat doughnuts all the time back home. My Mother's best friend Mrs. Thompson makes them and brings them over to us."

"This isn't a doughnut, (Laughing out loud) son, this is a bagel, here try one."

Mrs. Bergstein asked one of the porters to show me where the washroom was. I had never seen anything like it. The walls were made of marble, so were the floors and even the toilet seat and yes, a crystal chandelier for light right in the bathroom, wow!

"Thank you, Mrs. Bergstein." Now looking her in the face. "Can I go back to my 3rd class car now?"

"You will do nothing of the such! This is your seat for the rest of the trip, relax. I told you, I'm the boss on this train and you're my special guest!

Emmett, I want you to know that all whites are not the same. I hate the way that most of us treat your people, I don't like it one bit, and I fight on the Negroes defense at all times! Dr. King has my full support. That's probably why you can count the number of white friends I have on one hand.

Here, this is my business card, it's fancy and laminated, even hard for a 14-year-old boy to destroy, put it in your pocket. I do a lot of work for the N.A.A.C.P. If you or your mom ever get in trouble or need help, just give old Mrs. Bergstein a call. I'm not going to talk you to death, go to sleep Mr. Emmett Till, sweet dreams."

She gave me a soft pillow and wrapped a blanket around me, just like mom does. Sleep soon got a hold of me, and I was out for the count. When I woke up, the train had already made it to Mississippi. I looked over to the seat next to me, I was about to say good morning to Mrs. Bergstein, but she was gone.

In the seat was this letter:

Thank you, Mr. Emmett Till, I had a wonderful time talking with you. I will never forget you. Please tell your Mother that she has raised a fine young man. Maybe I'll see you in Money, Mississippi. One day, not in our lifetime, I truly believe whites and Colored will live in peace together, side-by-side. The day will come when a fine young man like you will grow up to be President of this great nation. Take care and have fun on your summer vacation, with much love:
Laura Bergstein

She even left $2.00 with the letter. I know that doesn't sound like much, but in 1955 for a 14-year-old it was plenty.

8

Money, Mississippi

Uncle Mose and my Cousin Simeon were waiting for me at the small train station, as I got off the train, he greeted me and shouted:

"There he is, the city boy from Chicago. Welcome to Money Mississippi Emmett! How was the ride? I was looking for you down at the Colored car, they said to find you here in first class with the white folks. Son, why the heck are you in the white folk's car, didn't Mamie tell you the do's and don'ts about Mississippi?"

"Yes, Uncle Mose, mom gave me the talk. This rich White lady let me ride on it, she's really – really rich. She gave me this business card."

"Let me take a look at that.......oh...she's a lawyer from the N.A.A.C.P., fancy card.

"You should have stayed where your mother said "

"Emmett, listen very close to me; you're in Mississippi now. Down here Colored boys and men don't come in contact with white girls or women – in no kind of way! Do you hear me, boy! You're gonna get yourself and those around you hung from a tree or thrown in the river. Do I make myself clear?" Don't say nothing to them, I mean nothing unless they ask you something!"

"Okay, yes Sir."

"I don't mean to be harsh on you boy, I'm just trying to send you back to Mamie the same way she sent you down here. Now let's go home and get something to eat, I know you must be hungry."

I didn't want to tell my Uncle that Mrs. Bergstein gave me all of that food. He was angry enough already. Simeon and I hopped into the horse-drawn buggy and went on to my Uncle's home.

Money is such a small town, it only took about 5 minutes to get there. He had an old hunting dog named Rex. That dog didn't like me at all. He barked and growled at me for most of the day.

"Don't worry Emmett, Uncle Mose explained, 'Rex does that to all strangers, he'll get used to you soon. Here, feed him this, make friends with him."

Mose gave me a chicken neck bone.

"Don't just stand there, go over and give it to him, don't be scared," he said. (laughing)

Simeon snatched the bone from my hand and gave it to Rex. He visits uncle Mose every year, the dog knows him well.

"That's all you had to do, scary cat. We're gonna do some rabbit hunting tomorrow and we need the dog to help us, you better hurry up and get used to him," Simeon warned.

"I don't care what you say, I don't like that dog," I said.

"Uncle Mose!" Simeon shouted. "Can I take Emmett into town to Bryant's grocery store? We want to get some skittles and iced tea."

Mose had already taken his shoes off and was resting in his favorite rocking chair. He put some snuff in his mouth, took a deep breath, and muttered: "Dammit, I got all comfortable, you boys settle down, ain't no need in going into town today."

Simeon whined and pleaded, "awww come on Uncle Mose. We'll be right back, you don't have to go with us. I know my way around town, plus, I won't let Emmett out of my sight, pleeeeeaseee."

"Okay," He declared. "Keep your eyes on him and stay out of trouble.

Go to the store and come right back! Ya hear!"

"We will – we will, come on Emmett, let's go.

" The south was as different from the north as night is to day.
We walked along a dirt road passing folks coming back and forth from town. Simeon pointed to a large tree and said:

"Last year, there were two Negro men hanging from this tree."

"You mean dead?" I replied.

Simeon whispered in my ear, "Yes they were dead."

"You weren't scared Simeon?"

"Almost every year, I see at least one black man hanging from a tree, and when we go fishing, we always see black bodies floating in the river."

"Stop lying to me Simeon, bodies in the river?"

"I'm not lying Emmett, it's the Klan, they the ones doing all the killing. Uncle Mose told me, they will hunt you down like a wild animal hunts for food. The Klan kills boys our age too. Come on, Bryant's grocery store is right around the corner."

When we made it to the store, Simeon had me stay on the outside while he went in to buy some skittles candy and iced tea. He came back out with two packages of skittles and two sodas.

"Simeon, where's my ice tea? I didn't want no soda!" I yelled.

"This soda is good. You'll like it, we always get this one, try it."
Simeon tried to explain.

"Take it home to Uncle Mose, I'll go back in myself and get the tea, I got my own money, see."

Bryant's grocery store was nothing more than a small wooden shack made into a store. I entered the store and looked around for the iced tea.

There was this young white woman behind the counter. She wore a name tag - "Carolyn Bryant."

"What are you looking for, boy?" She requested in a snappy voice.

"I'm looking for a can of iced tea Ma'am. My cousin came in and got the wrong drink."

"It's here in the cooler behind the counter with me. How many do you need?" She said in a stern voice, as to say hurry up, get what you want, and leave.

"Just one Ma'am, I only need one."

She snatched one out of the cooler, got a can opener, and punched a hole in the top of the can.

"That will be 7cents. You're new around here, I have never seen you before. Where are you from?"

Remembering what my mother said, while looking down to the floor, I mumbled while stuttering: "I'.....m frooom C.....hicagoooo Ma'aaaam."

I gave her a nickel and two rusty pennies and made my way out of there quick. As we were about to leave, a man in a brand-spanking-new 1955 Chevy Bel Air convertible pulled up in front of the store. It was baby-blue with shiny chrome all the way around. Simeon and I just stood there in awe. He had the radio up very loud. The man turned up the radio even louder, clenched his fist, and hit the dashboard hard, saying

. "DAMMIT! JUST LISTEN TO THIS NIGGA LOVER, I CAN'T STAND HIM..........I WISH SOMEONE WOULD JUST BLOW HIS FUCKING HEAD OFF!"

He got out of the car, slammed the door, and went inside the store. The radio was still on, so we just stood there and listened. It was President J.F. Kennedy speaking. I said to Simeon, "hey that's President Kennedy giving a speech, Mama loves him almost like Dr. King. She said he's the best President that ever was for us Colored folks."

President J.F. Kennedy speaking:

"My fellow Americans, ask not what your country can do for you! Ask what you can do for the poor Negroes in the ghettos of America! We war not against flesh and blood, but those who are in high places that want to keep Blacks and whites separate.

I have sent an executive order through congress. No longer will there be separate water fountains! No longer will there be separate schools! We shouldn't need armed military guards just to escort a harmless little Negro girl to class. Is this civilized behavior for the greatest and most 'Moral' country on the planet? We should be ashamed of ourselves! I've seen whites mocking the little girl with a noose around her neck. You mean to tell me that you want to hang and kill a little girl, only because she wants a proper education?

I just came from a funeral with Dr. King.

This is hard for me to say without crying (sobbing) - Four little Negro girls dead, just for attending church services. Grown white men with sheets on their heads, killing harmless little Black girls in church......what cowards! What is wrong with my white race? Why is it so hard for us to treat others the way we want to be treated? You wouldn't want a cross burning in your front yard, so why do it to others?

This must, and it will stop as long as I'm the Commander-in-Chief. I plan on being the President for a long time, so to those Jim Crow folks in the South, get used to seeing me, I'm not going anywhere! There's a new Sheriff in town, and I came to bust up your racist games!

The rights of all men are diminished when the rights of one man is taken away. How could the Negro fight over in Vietnam, and give his life for this land, only to come home to be hung from a tree or be burned alive because he was hungry and sat down at the 'wrong' lunch counter or wanted to vote?

How could a Negro woman, wanting to buy clothes for her children, be turned away from a major department store, only because she is not the right color? This is shameful!

How can I tell Fidel Castro, down in Cuba, that he is committing human rights violations when we are killing our own Colored citizen population by the hundreds every year? Most White Americans go to church every Sunday. What is the use of going to church, if we don't put into practice what we have learned?

Jackie and I had the great Billie Holiday as a special guest at the White House last night for the state dinner. She sang one of the most emotional songs I have ever heard, just listen to the lyrics.......excuse me – Tom could you please hand me the lyrics from last night.............oh yes – here it is, thank you Tom. When Mrs. Holiday got finished singing, there wasn't a dry eye in room, just listen to these words:

Southern trees bear strange fruit, Red blood on the leaves and red blood at the roots, Black male bodies swinging in the southern breeze,

Strange fruit hanging from the southern trees.
Pastoral scene of the majestic south,
The bulging eyes and the twisted mouth,
The fragrance of magnolias, sweet and fresh,
Then the sudden smell of burning Black flesh.

Here is ripe fruit for the crows to pluck,
For the rain to gather, for the wind to suck,
For the sun to decay, for the trees to drop,
Here is a strange and bitter crop.

President Kennedy Continues:

To Mrs. Rosa Parks: an American woman, who paid American money, to get on an American bus, traveling down an American street, to go to her American job, was taken to an American jail, by an American policeman, for sitting in a seat that she paid for. I humbly apologize to you, Mrs. Rosa Parks!

To Dr. King: when in Chicago, walking through Marquette Park, a public park, mind you, got hit in the head with a brick. You can hardly blame him for joining with Elijah Muhammad. I humbly apologize to you, Dr. King!

To the families of the three civil rights workers: Michael Henry Schwerner, Andrew Goodman and James Earl Chaney, who were lynched and killed by the Klan. I humbly apologize to your loved ones!

To the wife of Medgar Evers, a father and husband, shot down in his prime by wild white savages, I humbly apologize, Mrs. Myrlie Evers! I could go on and on about the everyday sins that are laid upon the Negroes in this country, but it would take several hours if not days. I fear, deep down in my soul, that the God I serve, is a just God, who will not look kindly on the White people of this land.

In my conclusion; I make a special appeal to Gov. Wallace of Mississippi. You have publicly made the statement: "Segregation today, segregation tomorrow, and segregation forever." You make it plain that you hate the Negro and you want Mississippi to have nothing to do with them.

We have found that the worse place for a Negro to live is in Money, Mississippi. The city of Money has more lynchings and murders than any other city in the United States! Governor Wallace, the Negro did not ask to be brought over here. They were forced out of their home, Africa. They are here to stay Mr. Wallace and there is nothing on God's green earth you can do about it!

Thank you for listening, God bless you, and God bless the United States of America.

9
The Deadly Whistle

The man came out of the grocery store, put what he purchased in the back seat of the car. He opened the trunk, got a towel out, and began to rub and shine on the car. A few minutes later, Mrs. Bryant came out and sat in a chair in front of the store to smoke a cigarette.

He turned to us and said: "Hey boys, Mrs. Bryant sure is a mighty fine White woman – ain't she?"

We just stood there scared and didn't say a word. He took a pistol from his waistband, started rubbing on it with the towel and said:

"I asked you boys a question. I said.......ain't Mrs. Bryant a fine looking woman?

ANSWER ME!!"

I looked at Simeon, his hands were shaking and he started to wet his pants. I then looked down to the ground and said nervously: "Yes Sir, if you say so Sir."

"Where are you from boy? You don't talk like you from here."

"I'm from Chicago Sir."

"Let's Pretend Mrs. Brant over there (Pointing to her with the nose of his gun) is a Chicago girl. What would you say to her?"

"Nothing Sir. I'm too young to talk to girls."

"Well, suppose – just suppose she started smiling at you and she blew a kiss at you? Would you whistle at her?" Let me hear how you whistle at those fine girls from Chicago."

He then pointed the gun directly at my head, saying: "Come on you little nigger boy, let's hear you whistle and make it loud!"

I put one index finger from my right hand, and one index finger from my left on each side of the inside of my mouth and howled out the loudest cat-call whistle' I have ever done.

Mrs. Bryant looked directly at me with her piercing razor-sharp blue eyes and shouted: "Did you just whistle at me little nigger boy?"

The man said to Mrs. Bryant: (snickering) "Looks like you got a secret admirer here Ma'am, a dark-skinned admirer."

Simeon grabbed my wrist and we ran as fast as we could back home. I have never seen that much fear in the eyes of my cousin.

He held my wrist so hard, I felt that my circulation was being cut off.

"Emmett, what the hell is wrong with you! You are trying to get us killed. Everybody knows that you don't whistle at White women in Mississippi. I thought you knew that!"

"Didn't you see that gun Simeon – he pointed it right at my head? What was I supposed to do – stand there and get shot?"

"He really wasn't going to shoot you, now you got us both in a whole lot of trouble. Wait until I tell Uncle Mose, I don't know what he's going to do to you when he finds out.

You are probably going to be on the first train in the morning going back to Chicago, that's after he beats the living daylights out of you.

I feel sorry for you Emmett. You see I didn't say anything. You should have kept your damn mouth shut!"

"Simeon, please don't tell Uncle Mose. I don't want to go back home, I just got here. That White lady might not say anything. Here, I'll give you $2.00 if you don't tell. Mose will tell mom, then when I get home I'll get another whipping. Come on Simeon, don't do me like that. I had no choice, that man had a gun on me."

"Okay, you can keep your money." He said reluctantly. "But you better hope that Mrs. Bryant doesn't tell her husband. If she does, he may come after all of us, including Uncle Mose. This is serious, very serious Emmett. They kill Negroes for stuff like this."

We made it home, Uncle Mose was asleep in the same chair he was in when we left. Simeon took those wet clothes off, washed up; I washed up and we went to bed.

10
Evil Enters The House

It must have been around 2:30 in the morning. Rex was barking like crazy, which woke me up from a very deep sleep. I heard Uncle Mose talking to someone at the front door.

"......Mr. Bryant please, He's just a kid, let me handle it. I'll beat that boy like nobody's business. He knows better than to do something stupid like that. Don't worry, I'll get him good."

The man said: "Those niggers from up north think they can just come to the south, whistle at a married white man's wife, and get away with it.......hell no!

I want that little nigger, and I want him now! Show me where he's at, or this house goes up in flames and every nigger in here dies!" (Holding a double-barreled sawed-off shotgun at Mose's face).

Uncle Mose shouted
(with strong emotion):

"Get the FUCK out of my house Bryant! You ain't taking that boy nowhere. I told you I'll discipline him myself!"

There was a scuffle between the two men. I woke Simeon up, shaking him like a rag doll. "Wake up Simeon – wake up! (Shaking him violently) Mrs. Bryant's husband is at the door – wake up!!"

All of a sudden we heard a very loud blast that sent a shock wave through the entire house. We just sat there in the bed looking at each other shaking and crying. We started crying out at the same time, "Uncle Mose -Uncle Mose – Uncle Mose!"

Everything got super quiet, then we heard footsteps slowly coming toward our bedroom. The doorknob slowly started to turn, then there was a high squeak sound from the door hinges as the door slowly opened.

A large scary looking white man, holding a shotgun in one hand and shining a bright flashlight at us with the other, came in. He had on a white dress shirt, splattered with bright red blood. He yelled out:"Which one of you is the nigga from Chicago that whistled at my wife!!"

He looked directly at me, pointing with his index finger dripping with blood, and said:"You boy – what's your name?"

Stuttering got a hold of my throat like a king cobra choking on its prey. "M....y naaaammme Is E....mm......ett Sir."

"Yeah, you da one." He yelled out. "Put your clothes on, we are going on a little trip."

I put my clothes back on. Then he grabbed me by the back of my collar, pulling me backward, my heels sliding on the blood-stained floor leaving two red lines along the way. As he was pulling me, he bent down and whispered in my ear, "You're gonna wish you never whistled at my wife, boy. Your Uncle got it easy....he died instantly.....but you...I'm gonna torture you for a long time before I kill you."

He pulled me pass Uncle Mose's body, blood was everywhere, even on the ceiling. The right side of his face was blown completely off. I thought to myself; Mose was a very brave man, he didn't just hand me over to this beast, he stood his ground like a man, and died like a man!

Mr. Bryant's first name was Roy and his brother's name was Milam. Milam was serving as a look-out, waiting outside in Roy's pickup truck. "Roy." Milam whispered. "You sure you got the right one....are you sure?"

"I'm sure. Let's go." Roy whispered back.

Milam looked worried. "What about the other one? He's gonna rat us out. We should get him too."

"Even if he does Milam, our childhood friend Jake is the police chief and Daddy's friend Curt is the Judge. white men don't go to jail for killing niggers my brother - never did - never will. Don't worry, when we get finished with this Chicago boy, his cousin won't be saying a damn thing to anyone."

"Where are we gonna kill him it at Roy? Let's just tie him to the back of the truck and drag the little nigger to death. That would be more fun." Milam said. (Grinning from ear-to-ear)

They hog-tied me, put tape around my mouth and threw me in the back of the truck. I could hear them talking and laughing.

"Hey Roy." Milam said, "Don't you think congratulations are in order?"

"Congratulations for what brother?"

"This boy Emmett will make our 50th nigger kill since our first one when I was 17 and you were 15. His Uncle was the 49th and this one makes it 50."

"You know, the other ones I really don't remember, but your first nigger kill you never forget. Back in Dad's day, you could just hang a nigger or burn him on sight without having to find somewhere to hide to do it.

Daddy had it easy, he and his Klan friends killed over 250 in his lifetime. That man taught us everything we know about killing these no-good darkies. He was a good man Milam, I really miss him."

"You know, I think you're right, so this is number 50 huh. Wow, I wasn't keeping count, but you may be right, it's been quite a few, but we never killed one this young. Yes, my brother, congratulations are in order."

I could hear two cans being popped open, they hit the cans together and said at the same time: "TOAST."

"Make a left turn here, we're gonna take him to the old barn on Center St. He can scream as loud as he wants and no one within 5 miles would hear anything."

11
The Lynching

    For some reason, a calm came over me and I stopped crying.
Memories of what Mama told me about what white folks did to us in slavery came to my mind, the speech that I heard from The Hon. Elijah Muhammad, and my entire childhood started flashing by in my head; even all the way back to my birth.

    I started praying to God right there from the back of the truck, as it was bouncing up and down from the uneven clay-dirt road.

(please bow your head, and pray with me)

Dear Lord — God. I thank you for the life that you gave me; I thank you for my Mother and Father; Lord, I thank you for my brave Uncle; I thank you for allowing me to breathe your air, for allowing me to walk on your earth. I don't know the purpose of this my Lord, but to you is my eventual return. Let it end quickly my Lord, don't let them torture me, because torture is worse than outright slaughter. How long oh Lord Jesus - How long will this evil exist among my people? I began crying again.

(Sobbing profusely)

Roy cut the ropes from my hands and ankles, then ripped the tape off my mouth. He tossed me out of the truck to the ground and proceeded to drag me into the barn by my left ankle, which still had a piece of rope attached to it. There was a large wooden vertical beam in the middle of the barn. He stood me up against it and tied me to it.

Milam came in holding an axe in one hand and a long sharp ice pick in the other. He put them on the floor next to me and went back out to the truck.

I started crying out as loud as I have ever cried out: "HELP ME -HELP – OH LORD – SOMEBODY HELP – OH MY GOD – HELP ME!!"

Roy came up to me, face-to-face, put his nose on my nose, tip-to-tip, looked me straight in the eyes, made his voice deeper than it actually was, and said:

"Shout as loud as you want little nigger boy......ain't no one for miles around, plus, I like it when you scream.........so go ahead."

Milam came back in, this time he had a long 12in butcher knife in one hand and a pistol in the other. Once again, he put them on the floor at my feet. He said to his brother, "You can have the honor of going first brother, choose your weapon."

Roy picked up the butcher knife and said to me, "so you like to whistle at white women huh. You wouldn't be able to whistle if you didn't have a tongue........Hey Milam, can a person whistle if they don't have a tongue?"

"I don't think so Roy." Milam replied. Maybe you better fix that for him. Remember how we dissected frogs in school, you know what to do. Didn't you get an 'A' in that class?"

He picked up a pair of rusty pliers that were on a workbench. I kept my mouth closed tight. Roy said, "open your mouth now boy – OPEN IT!" I kept it closed. He told Milam to take my pants off, now tears were running down my face like never before.

Milam put the cold knife next to my private parts and said: "My brother said open your mouth boy, and when you do, open it wide."

I started crying out to my Mama - "MA..MAAAAAA!" and opened my mouth wide, tears flowing into my mouth like Niagara Falls. Roy took the pliers and pulled my tongue out, he grabbed the butcher knife from Milam and cut my tongue out. I gagged from the flow of blood going down my throat.

Next, he put the pistol on the side of my head and shot me point-blank through the head. At that point, my soul left the body. Somehow, I knew I was dead, but I was looking down, seeing everything that was going on.

Milam picked up the axe, took a long deep breath, and with full force, chopped my skull in half from ear-to-ear. He then took the ice pick and gauged my eyes out, leaving one eye hanging on my cheek. Lastly, he carved three lines into the bridge of my nose, saying: "I always leave these signature marks on my nigger kills."

They put the pants back on my lifeless body, threw me inside the pickup truck, drove about 3 miles down the road to the Tallahatchie River, and parked on the bridge.

The Tallahatchie is where Uncle Mose said they find most of the lynched Negroes. When we got there, Milam took an old heavy cotton gin fan, tied it around my neck with barbed wire, and threw me into the river from the bridge. They drove off in the truck with my blood streaming from the back, leaving a long red trail.

12
A Mother Searches For Her Son

My Mother came here and joined with other family members and friends to search for me. The authorities found many other Black male bodies around town, some in the river, some hanging from trees, and some that have been burned alive, all castrated, but they didn't find me.

I was in the watery grave for 3 days before a Father, fishing with his son, got his fish line caught in the barbed wire around my neck and noticed arms and legs coming to the surface. Soon, a bunch of police and newspaper folks came to see my mangled body being pulled from the river. Mama wasn't there at the time.

She went to the coroner to identify me, but they wouldn't let her see me. They told her my body was messed up and she wouldn't be able to bear the sight of me.

The only thing they did was give her the ring from my finger, the one Daddy gave me, and Mrs. Bergstein's laminated business card that was still in my left pocket.

The coroner said I would be cremated in 2 days. Mom still wasn't satisfied, she demanded to see my actual body. She only wanted some kind of closure and those white folks in Mississippi were making sure she didn't get it.

Mama looked at the business card and noticed that Mrs. Bergstein was a lawyer. She found a payphone and called her.

Mrs. Till:
Hello, may I speak with Mrs. Bergstein, please.

Mrs. Bergstein:
Hello, this is she. How can I help you?

Mrs. Till:
My name is Mrs. Mamie Till, I have your business card. Do you know my son Emmett?

Mrs. Bergstein:
Oh yes, I most certainly do know that fine young man. I met him on the train traveling here to Money, Mississippi. I told him to tell you how much I admire him and you. How is he.......is everything okay?

Mrs. Till:
I am calling you from Money, I'm here now. Mrs. Bergstein, you haven't heard the news?

Mrs. Bergstein:
I just flew back in from a short business meeting in Canada. You're here – in Money, Mississippi – right now? Emmett told me you were in Chicago.........what news, what are you talking about?

Mrs. Till:
I have some very sad news: Mrs. Bergstein, Emmett is missing, and his Uncle is dead.

Mrs. Bergstein:
WHAT! - WHAT DID YOU JUST SAY! HE'S MISSING........WHAT
DO YOU MEAN HE'S MISSING!!

Mrs. Till:
I just got down here today. I was told that Emmett supposedly whistled at some white lady named Mrs. Bryant, and from what I was told, two white guys came to Mose's house, shot him and took Emmett. They said my baby was found 3 days later floating in the Tallahatchie River.

The coroner said they have his body and they were going to cremate him in two days. Mrs. Bergstein, they won't let me see the body to identify him. (Weeping) I don't even know if it's Emmett or not, he may be alive somewhere. Can you please help me find my son? I don't have a lot of money, can you help me, please?

Mrs. Bergstein:
Oh my God! (Crying) Mrs. Till, I am so sorry........I hope those racist bastards didn't do anything to that young boy. Don't worry, I promise you, on my life – I will find out what happened to Emmett and his Uncle. Don't worry about paying me anything - this is personal! I'm doing this Pro Bono. I fell in love with little Emmett the moment I saw him! Don't worry, I'm on this – in 25 years and I have never lost a case. You and your family are in my prayers. Oh, yes........I almost forgot, my office is 1897 E. Whaley Rd. Where are you staying?

Mrs.Till:
Thank you so much, I'm glad Emmett made such an impression on you, he does that to everyone. I'll be staying at the Holiday Inn on SunnySide Rd. Room 111.

Mrs. Bergstein:
I'm paying for the room Mrs. Till, stay as long as you need. Order as much food as you want. I got the tab, and don't try to talk me out of it! Good Bye.

The next day Mrs. Bergstein was able to get a government court order to stop my cremation. She told Mama to please let her view the body first. The medical examiner gave her a 3pm appointment to view the remains. She walked into the frigid examination room, with cold smoke coming from every breath she took.

The coroner said, "he's over there, he's the last one on the right. The one with the lion tattoo. Are you satisfied?"

"What's this?" She shouted, looking puzzled, "where is the boy?"

The coroner looked at her and said in a very calm- relaxed voice, "you're looking at the boy lady, that's him. We get Negroes pulled from the river all the time, that's how they look, frankly, I've seen worse. At least his head is still attached."

She put both hands on each side of her face and shouted - "WHAT THE HELL!! What did those demons do to this precious boy! It doesn't even look human........it looks like some kind of sea monster or something, Oh my God!"

The examiner looked at the lawyer and said, "now you see why we didn't want his mother or those nosy news reporters to see him – do you agree?"

"No, I don't agree, Sir." Stomping her feet, "Hell no, you just didn't want the public to see what your two friends did to this innocent youth in Money, Mississippi. His mom is on the way here now, after that, the whole world will know! Those bastards will pay dearly for this!"

Mrs. Bergstein stayed there next to me until Mama arrived. She didn't want the coroner to try anything like cremating me "by mistake."

13
A Mother's Grief

Mama arrived exactly 1hr later. Mrs. Bergstein greeted her at the front door. Mom said to her, "why are we stopping here, let's go inside – is it him? - is my baby in there?"

The lawyer just stood there, holding both of Mama's hands, looking her straight in the eyes, and said: "Mamie, sweetheart, I couldn't really tell if that was Emmett or not, I just couldn't make out any features. Does he have any special markings on his body?"

"Yeah." She eagerly said. "He's got a mole right here (Pointing to her upper chest) and he's got a tattoo of a loin on his upper right arm."

Mrs. Bergstein went from looking Mama directly in the eyes, to slowly looking down to the floor, covering her face with both hands, and started crying. Mama pushed her out of the way and ran inside the cold examination room.

The examiner screamed -"Wait lady, you can't just go in there unescorted, come back here!"

It was too late, she busted through the stainless steel double doors. There were five other Black male bodies in there with me. She hollered out in an extra loud voice, "WHERE IS MY BABY! - WHERE IS MY BABY!"

She went down the line, looking at each body, mine was the last one. After she finished looking at the others, Mama looked in my direction and started walking towards me in slow motion.

My right arm was hanging out from under the covering, she saw the lion tattoo – at the same time, the coroner was pulling the covering off of me.

She just fell to the floor, on both knees, pounding on the floor with her fists, crying out: "OH MY LORD JESUS, WHAT DID THEY DO TO MY BABY- LORD JESUS, THEY DIDN'T HAVE TO DO MY BABY LIKE THAT – THEY DIDN'T HAVE TO DO MY BABY LIKE THAT! OH GOD!!!"

-Mama passed out-

Roy and Milam were eventually arrested, held for about 1 hour and set free. The trial date was set for Thursday, September 19th at 12 noon. The jury consisted of 12 men, all white, mostly over 50. The Judge's name was Curt Swango.

14

The Trial
Day of the Trial

Judge Curt Swango's instructions to the jury:

"Members of the Jury. You must decide on the facts and exclusively from the evidence alone. It is up to you, and you alone to decide what happened in this case. Based only on the evidence presented in this trial. Do not let bias, prejudice, sympathy, public opinion, or public influence sway your decision. Bias includes race, religion, gender, and age.

If you hear something said by one of the lawyers that conflicts with what I said, just remember what I say supersedes the lawyers. You must follow the law as I have explained it – even if you disagree with it. A defendant is presumed innocent until proven guilty beyond a reasonable doubt. We will now hear an opening statement from the prosecution. Mrs. Bergstein, please proceed."

Attorney Bergstein:
Good morning your honor and gentlemen of the jury. My name is Laura Bergstein. As you were told during jury selection, this is the case of Mrs. Mamie Till – Bradley vs. Roy and Milam Bryant. This isn't just a case about Till vs. Bryant, it's the story about a 14 year-old boy – a child named Emmett who was brutally lynched and murdered.

I want you to close your eyes for a moment and picture in your mind a black boy born July 25, 1941. He lived every day of his life with his mother in a nice quiet household in Chicago. He loved his mother, and she loved her only son. She worked hard for her son, sometimes working two jobs at a time. When she would put him to sleep at night, both Mother and son would say their prayers together.

Emmett did everything that a normal 14-year-old boy would do, like playing basketball, baseball, swimming and even winning top honors as a Boy Scout. He also sang in the choir at the local church. Emmett got straight "A's" in school. Here is a copy of his last report card.

Yes, gentlemen of the jury, today we will learn that a normal – loving 14-year-old boy, was stalked – kidnapped – brutally beaten and lynched. This beautiful young man (Holding up a large photo of Emmett and his Mother hugging) was savagely mutilated like a pack of wild wolves, tearing apart the flesh of a helpless animal.

While in college, I took a class that studied the behavior of wolf packs. It's no different from how the Klan and the Bryant brothers operate when they see a helpless Black man or boy that they want to devour.

First, wolves locate the prey: Just like the Bryant brothers did to Emmett.

Second, they stalk what they intend to kill: Just like the Bryant brothers did with Emmett.

Third, wolves make the final encounter: Just like Milam and Roy did when they forced their way into Mr. Moses Wight's home – killing him in cold blood, then kidnapping and murdering Emmett. Folks, that young boy didn't have the luxury to die instantly.......no, he was tortured for hours before he died.

That kind of torture wasn't even done to enemy soldiers on foreign battlefields, it's against international law – let alone doing it to a child!

Members of the jury – do you know what it feels like for your world to end? Just ask Mamie Till, she'll tell you what it's like because she knows.

The evidence, in this case, is overwhelming folks. Blood still in the bed of the truck, blood tracks that match the shoes of both brothers. Blood, everywhere folks, we have the owner of the local cleaners, who will describe how he found blood all over the Bryant brother's clothing. This is far beyond responsible doubt.

Emmett did absolutely nothing to deserve what happened to him. He was said to have whistled at Mrs. Bryant, who was working at the store that day.

Gentlemen, we all have children that like to whistle, is that some kind of crime? Should a boy die just for whistling?
Thank You.

Attorney Carlton for the defense makes his opening statement:

Thank you, your honor. Members of the jury, my name is Sid Carlton. I am here to represent these two fine outstanding citizens of Money, Mississippi; Roy and Milam Bryant. There have been a lot of unfounded accusations thrown at my clients. Actually, better words would be outright lies. When all the evidence is shown, we will see that these men are innocent of all charges. We still don't know if the body pulled from the river was actually Emmett Till.........is he still alive? - We just don't know. That's doubt folks – pure doubt.

Yes, my clients went to the home, they questioned the boy and took him back home. The blood that the prosecution claims came from two deer kills. The Bryant brothers go hunting quite often. Notice she didn't say it was Emmett's blood – she just said there was a lot of blood.

Well, what do you expect from two guys trying to cut up a 500-pound deer from the truck bed – you get a lot of blood.

(the jury starts laughing)

As for Mose Wight, our condolences go out to the family, but my clients had nothing to do with his murder. Folks, Bryant's grocery store has been in operation for the past 50 years, this is a family-owned business. It's also one of the few stores around that serve both white and Black customers. That alone proves that this fine family has no hatred for Negroes.

Sitting over here (Pointing to his left) we have the families of Roy and Milam Bryant. Look in the green eyes of Milam's cute little daughter and tell her that you're going to send her daddy away to jail for a murder that he didn't commit.

Now folks, look into the beautiful blue eyes of Roy's pregnant wife and tell her that she won't see her husband again for the next 20 years. We have too much doubt here folks. That mountain of doubt means only one thing. By law, you must find them not guilty. Thank you.

Judge Swango:
Mr. Milam Bryant, would you please take the stand.

Milam Bryant:
Yes, Sir. Your honor

Judge Swango:
Please put your left hand on the Bible, lift your right hand and repeat after me – I, 'say your name,' do solemnly swear that the testimony that I am about to give is the truth, the whole truth, and nothing but the truth, so help me God.

Milam Bryant:
I, Milam J. Bryant, do solemnly swear that the testimony that I am about to give is the truth, the whole truth, and nothing but the truth, so help me God.

Judge Swango:
Please have a seat, Mr. Bryant. Mrs. Bergstein, you may now question the defendant.

Attorney Bergstein:
Mr. Bryant, You have already admitted that you and your brother did in fact go to Mr. Moses Wright's home to see Emmett, is that true?

Milam Bryant:
Yes Ma'am that is true, but we didn't kill him.

Attorney Bergstein:
When you got there, you were already very angry.... is that true?

Milam Bryant:
No Ma'am, I wasn't angry at all, I just wanted to question the boy about what he said to my wife, that's all. I asked Mr. Wright if I could talk to the boy and he said yes.

Attorney Bergstein:
Please tell us what happened after that.

Milam Bryant:
Well, Mr. Wright directed me to where Emmett's room was and I asked if he was the one that whistled at my wife. The boy said yes. I asked him to put on some clothes, he did and we sat in the truck and talked. Then we drove less than a mile away and I brought him right back. We had two deers in the back of the truck, that's where all the blood came from.

Attorney Bergstein:
Mr. Bryant, I'm just going to ask you straight out – did you and your brother murder Mr. Wright and Emmett Till?

Milam Bryant:
Ma'am, why would I want to kill them, I had no reason to kill that old man, and certainly not a child.

Attorney Bergstein:
Sir, I didn't ask if you had a reason to kill them, I asked if you did kill them – that's either yes or no Mr. Bryant!

Attorney Carlton:
Objection Your Honor, she is being too harsh in questioning the witness.

Judge Swango:
Sustained, counselor please be less harsh when you ask the questions.

Attorney Bergstein:
Mr. Bryant, did you and your brother kill Emmett Till? Let me remind you that you are still under oath.

Milam Bryant:
No Ma'am, we did not.

Attorney Bergstein:
So, all of that blood you say was from some game that you guys killed. Do you usually visit a person's home with your shoes and clothing dripping with blood?

Milam Bryant:
No, not usually, but this time we did, we were in a hurry.

Attorney Bergstein:
There was also a lot of blood found at the barn on Center street. Do you know anything about that?

Milam Bryant:
No Ma'am, I don't know anything about that.

Attorney Bergstein:
Did you also know that tire tracks leading to and from the barn match the tires on your truck?

Attorney Carlton:
Objection Your Honor, there must be hundreds of trucks in Mississippi that may have the same kind of tires!

Judge Swango:
Sustained, Mrs. Bergstein, please ask your questions in a different manner.

Attorney Bergstein:
Mr. Bryant, did you ever drive to that barn at any time?

Milam Bryant:
No Ma'am, I have not.

Attorney Bergstein:
Your Honor, I need to ask these questions to find out who killed that young man and his Uncle. His Mother is sitting over there grief-stricken, and she needs and wants justice for her family.

Attorney Carlton:
You have no right to treat my client like that.

Judge Swango:
Both of you approach the bench now! Listen to me, the two of you are acting like little children arguing in a play lot, you're making me sick. Stop it right now! That's all I have to say.

Attorney Carlton:
Yes, Sir. Your Honor, but she acts like she has some kind of personal connection to that Negro boy.

As the two attorneys were returning to their seats, Mr. Carlton whispered in the ear of Mrs. Bergstein - "what are you, some king of nigger-lover or something?"

Mrs. Bergstein whispered back in his ear - "go to hell – you racist bastard."

Attorney Bergstein:
Mr. Bryant, this is what I believe happened that night.

Attorney Carlton:
Objection Your Honor, she can't say what she thinks or what she believes happened, she must prove her case with actual facts.

Judge Swango:
Overruled, please continue counselor.

Attorney Bergstein:
Thank you, Your Honor, as I was saying, I believe that your wife told you that a little nigger boy came into the store that day and got fresh with her. You got pissed off, got your brother, and went looking for the boy. Next, you drove to Mr. Wight's home, went inside where a confrontation between you and Mr. Wright took place. You pulled out a shotgun, shot him in the face point-blank, and then went looking for Emmett.

You then went into the room where Simeon and Emmett were sleeping. Sir, you and Roy kidnapped the youth, tied him up, and threw the boy in the back of the truck. The actual murder took place at the barn on Center Street. You and Roy lynched that boy didn't you Milam!! The boy was tortured for hours, wasn't he!!

Attorney Carlton:
Objection Your Honor, Objection! Just listen to her, she can't........

Jude Swango:
Overruled, continue Mrs. Bergstein.

Attorney Bergstein:
You and Roy also castrated that child, tied a cotton gin fan around his neck with barbed wire, and tossed him in the river, didn't you...........didn't you?

Milam Bryant:
I told you, we didn't kill the boy.

Attorney Bergstein:
You probably lynched that poor child while he was still alive, didn't you? Mr. Bryant, one day I sat down and had a long conversation with an Ex – Klan member.

Do you want to know what he told me? He said that the reason they castrate Black men and boys is because they are afraid of genetic annihilation. They are aware of one simple fact: if a Black man mixes with a white woman, the child won't come out white, it will be Black. If a white man mixes with a Black woman, the child will also be Black. That's how strong the Black blood is. The dominant Black sperm will always overwhelm the recessive white sperm. That's what you are afraid of Sir. And that's why you castrated that child. You-In your sick and perverted mind, and all whites that do that to Black men, thinking that you are somehow preserving the white race. Am I correct Mr. Bryant?

Milam Bryant:
I have no idea what you're talking about lady.

Attorney Carlton:
Objection Your Honor!! - that has nothing to do with this case.

Judge Swango:
Overruled, she's not hurting the case by telling us this, please continue counselor.

Attorney Bergstein:
I have no further questions, Your Honor.

15

The Other Bad News
Judge Swango:

Before we proceed, I have a very important message that just came by way of telegram. I was going to wait until we were fully finished here, but it's marked 'urgent message directly from the White House.' This type of message goes out to all judges and courts and must be opened immediately to the public. Bailiff, please hand me the letter so that I may read it. Let me take a look at it first......................Oh my God! This is a message directly from President Kennedy. (Taking a drink of water and clearing his throat) It reads as follows:

Good afternoon my fellow Americans, this is your President. I have some very saddening news for all of you, and I think sorrowful news for all of our U.S. citizens and people who love peace all over the world, and that is that Dr. King was shot and killed today in Memphis, Tennessee.

A very loud sad-mournful noise came from the Blacks, along with cheering from the whites.

Dr. King devoted his life to love and justice between fellow human beings. He died in the cause of that endeavor. In this difficult hour – in this difficult time for America, it's perhaps best to ask what kind of a nation we are, and what path we want to move in.

For those of you who are Black – considering the fact that there was a white man who pulled the trigger – you can be filled with bitterness, and hatred, and desire retaliation.

We can move in that direction as a country, being more polarized – Black people amongst Blacks, and white amongst whites, filled with hatred toward one another. Or we can make an attempt, as Dr. King did, to understand and to comprehend, and replace that aggression, that stain of bloodshed that has spread across our land, with compassion and love for our fellow man.

For those of you who are Black, and are enticed to fill, or be filled with hatred and suspicion of the injustice of such an act, against all white people, I would only say that I can likewise feel in my own heart the same kind of feeling. A white man also tried to kill me, and my brother Robert.

We have to make an effort in the United States, we have to make an effort to understand, to get beyond, and go beyond these challenging times.

What we need is not division; what we need is not hatred; what we need in the United States is not hostility and lawlessness. We need love and wisdom, and sympathy toward one another, the feeling of justice toward those who still suffer within our country, whether they be white or whether they be Black.

We've had difficult times in the past. And we will have difficult times in the days henceforth. It is not the end of hatred; it is not the end of lawlessness, and it's not the end of disorder. I am not so naive to believe such. But the vast majority of white people and the vast majority of Black people in this country want to live together, want to improve the quality of our life, and want justice for all human beings that abide here in the U.S.A.

Dr. King was a great man, a husband, a father, a pastor, and a leader. I will now read a shortlist of the great things this man of God has done.

1. The Montgomery Bus Boycott.
2. Founding of the Southern Christian Leadership Conference. (SCLC)
3. The Birmingham Movement – The March on Washington.
4. The massive voter registration movement.
5. Education programs – School integration.
6. The poor people's campaign In Memphis
7. A call for the end of the war in Vietnam.
8. Winning the Nobel Peace Prize.
9. The Freedom Rides in Georgia.
10. Founder of the sit-in movement.
11. Helping the sanitation workers in Chicago.

Thank you for your time, May God bless you, and May God bless the United States of America.

16
"The Verdict"

The jury came back from recess, deliberating for only 10 min. They came back with 15 words that stuck a dagger in Mama's heart:
"We, the jury, find the defendants not guilty on all charges - so say we all." Mama broke down to the floor on both knees, put her face in the palms of both hands, and just wept. Just like the Bible - Jesus wept - Mama wept, she wept for the verdict and she wept for Dr. King.

News of Dr. King's assassination reached every ghetto in America. Riots began to break out everywhere. The government dispatched 1,300armed troops, including the National Guard to the affected areas. Many innocent Blacks were killed.

Blacks were breaking into white-owned stores taking everything that they could grab. The police were greatly outnumbered and couldn't control the people. Many cities were left in ashes and rubble. Mama had to wait a week before my body was transported back to Chicago for the funeral. When my body finally made it back home, Mama contacted A.A. Rayner Funeral home, located at 41st and Cottage Grove.

The funeral director asked mom if she wanted to have a closed-casket funeral. She told him absolutely not, she wanted the entire world to see what those devils did to me. Thousands of people came to see me. I didn't realize just how much my people actually loved me. Most of the women that saw me usually broke down and had to be escorted out by a nurse.

My eulogy was done by a close family friend
Ossie Davis:

Brothers and Sisters, Emmett lived an awesome life, even though it was rather short. He was a great friend of mine; he was the kind of friend that stood by you when you needed somebody to be there. What is it that we recollect when we think of Emmett?

I think everyone who knew him very well would agree with me on this, it was his sense of humor. He was the kind of person that would make everyone laugh so hard that they'd end up crying. That is what I will truly miss about Emmett. He could make you laugh when you're really sad. He would cheer you up when he knew you just had a bad day. That's the trademark of Emmett.

He always wanted to make people happy. Emmett's death was sudden. I remember when I heard the news, I simply could not believe it. He was so young, but as it slowly occurred to me, I have realized that Emmett indeed lived his life wonderfully. Emmett was well-loved and he had done so many things on earth and I'm sure he'll do much more in heaven.

I will forever be grateful to have known Emmett and his wonderful Mother. All the memories I have shared with them will forever be cherished and remembered. Emmett will eternally live in my heart. In our hearts forever. He is in heaven now, and we are here at his funeral. This is not the time for us to grieve his death, but it's our time to celebrate his life. We must never forget Emmett. He never wanted to see people cry.

He wanted to make everyone happy. So at this moment when we are about to lay his body to rest, let's all think back and remember how Emmett touched our lives. How he made us laugh, and how good Emmett was as a person. I know that it will be very difficult for my long-time friend

Mamie, to go forward without her son Emmett in her life. However, I also know that Emmett would not want us to be overwhelmed with sadness. He was a very strong and positive young man, he would always look for the best in any situation, and would want us to do the same.

Let's remember Emmett for all of his great qualities and appreciate the time we spent with him. We should make sure that his memory lives on in all of us for as long as we live because our funeral day is also coming. Emmett was like a fruit that was plucked from the tree before it had time to get ripe. If we love the fruit, we must also love the tree that produced the fruit, his mother!

(Wiping tears from his eyes and looking directly at Mrs. Till sitting in the front row.)

Mamie...........I want you to know we all love you. Again, this is not the moment or time for us to shed our tears, although that's exactly what I'm doing; but we should all be thankful that we were given the chance to have known this young man named Emmett, also known as "Bobo." (Mrs. Till smiling)

We should all be thankful that a strong Black woman named Mamie Till gave birth to this wonderful Black brother. He will forever be missed, but I know, at the right time, I will meet Emmett again. We will all meet Emmett again, and he'll make us laugh again once more.
I say goodbye, to our fallen Black soldier - goodbye............and may God hold you in the palm of his hands.
Thank You

17
"The Confession"

J.W. Milam and Roy Bryant finally confessed to Look Magazine on January 24, 1956. Since they were acquitted of Emmett's murder, they knew that they could not be tried again for the same thing. Surprisingly, during the trial, one of the members of the jury had voted twice to convict the Bryant brothers, before giving up and joining the majority. The brothers, who were found to be Klan Members, were paid over $4,000 for their participation in the article.

**The article was titled:
"The Shocking Story of Approved Killing in Mississippi."**

Milam and Roy detailed how they murdered Till, then tossing his body in the Tallahatchie River with a heavy cotton-gin fan attached with barbed wire to his neck to weigh him down.

His decomposed body was found three days later on August 31 st. Milam and Bryant were never brought to justice and both later died of cancer.

Emmett Till's grave site is located at Burr Oak Cemetery 4400 W. 127th t, Alsip, IL

18
Quotes About Emmett Till

"When people saw what had happened to my son, men stood up who had never stood up before."

-Mamie Till-Mobley

"I thought about Emmett Till, and I could not go back. My legs and feet were not hurting, that is a stereotype. I paid the same fare as others, and I felt violated. I was not going back."

-Rosa Parks, civil rights activist

"I think the picture in Jet magazine showing Emmett Till's mutilation was probably the greatest media product in the last forty or fifty years because that picture stimulated a lot of interest and anger on the part of blacks all over the country."

-Congressman Charles Diggs

"Emmett Till and I were about the same age. A week after he was murdered . . . I stood on the corner with a gang of boys, looking at pictures of him in the black newspapers and magazines. In one, he was laughing and happy. In the other, his head was swollen and bashed in, his eyes bulging out of their sockets and his mouth twisted and broken. His mother had done a bold thing. She refused to let him be buried until hundreds of thousands marched past his open casket in Chicago and looked down at his mutilated body. I felt a deep kinship to him when I learned he was born the same year and day I was. My father talked about it at night and dramatized the crime. I couldn't get Emmett out of my mind."

-**Muhammad Ali**

After the inhumane murder of her son, Mamie Till continued to live in Chicago as a public school teacher for 24 years, and never stopped speaking publicly on Emmett's behalf.

She died on January 6, 2003

At the age of 81.

19

Photos of other lynchings

The Lynching Of Will Brown Omaha, 1919

Will Brown was accused of raping a white woman. He was brought to the Douglas County Courthouse to await trial. He never had the opportunity to prove his innocence. On the night of September 28, a mob numbering <u>10 thousand</u> converged on the courthouse. Setting the building on fire. The mayor tried to intervene, but he was beaten unconscious. When the mob got their hands on Will Brown, he was beaten, dragged by a rope from a car, shot, and burned to death on the street. Notice the smiling faces, even a young boy.

Laura and her son, L.D. Nelson

(born 1878 and 1897) were lynched on May 25, 1911, near Okemah, the county seat of Okfuskee County, Oklahoma. Laura, her husband Austin, their teenage son L.D., and possibly their child had been taken into custody after George Loney, Okemah's deputy sheriff, and three others arrived at the Nelsons' home on May 2, 1911, to investigate the theft of a cow.

The son shot Loney, who was hit in the leg and bled to death; Laura was reportedly the first to grab the gun and was charged with murder, along with her son. Her husband pleaded guilty to larceny and was sent to the relative safety of the state prison in McAlester, while their son was held

in the county jail in Okemah and Laura in a cell in the nearby courthouse to await trial. At around midnight on May 24, Laura and her son were kidnapped from their cells by a group of between a dozen and 40 men; the group included Charley Guthrie (1879-1956), the father of folk singer Woody Guthrie (1912-1967), according to a statement given in 1977 by the former's brother. *The Crisis*, the magazine of the National Association for the Advancement of Colored People, said in July 1911 that Laura was raped, then she and L.D. were hanged from a bridge over the North Canadian River. According to some sources, Laura had a baby with her at the time, who one witness said survived the attack.

The 1920 Duluth Lynchings

The **1920 Duluth lynchings** occurred on June 15, 1920, when three African American circus workers were attacked and lynched by a mob in Duluth, Minnesota. Rumors had circulated that six African Americans had raped and robbed a teenage girl.

A physician's examination subsequently found no evidence of rape or assault. The killings shocked the country, particularly for their occurrence in the northern United States, although four earlier lynchings had occurred in Minnesota. In 2003, the city of Duluth erected a memorial to the murdered workers.

Thankful and Grateful to Have You as a Customer!

I Hope You Enjoy Your Book! Please Share On Social Media.

Ernest Muhammad

messagetotheblackman.com

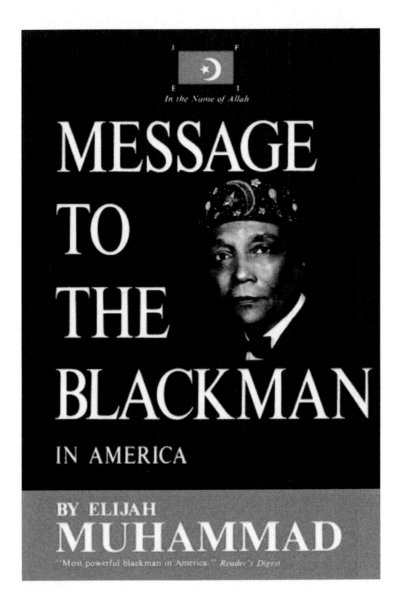

In the Name of Allah

MESSAGE TO THE BLACKMAN

IN AMERICA

BY ELIJAH MUHAMMAD

"Most powerful blackman in America." *Reader's Digest*

Printed in Great Britain
by Amazon

16428078R00095